Turner Justice

Dan Decker

Published by Grim Archer Media, 2020.

This is a work of fiction. Similarities to real people, places, or events are entirely coincidental.

TURNER JUSTICE

First edition. April 10, 2020.

Copyright © 2020 Dan Decker.

Written by Dan Decker.

For my family.

The Mugger

1

It was already dark when I came out of the courthouse, stuffing a file into my briefcase as I walked down the street. I had been at the court all afternoon and then got stuck in an impromptu meeting with Frank Ward, a prosecuting attorney. We had tried to hammer out a plea deal for a client who had got caught trying to sell his personal stash of meth after he decided to go clean.

Or so he claims.

I didn't believe it and neither did Frank, so perhaps that was why my client was telling it to anybody who would listen. He'd told the story to me three times today but that hardly mattered now as we haggled over how many years he was going to spend in prison.

I growled under my breath, frustrated that my client had wanted to sleep on the offer. I'd badgered Frank down to below what he should have offered because this was a small matter to him and he just wanted it off of his desk.

It was a good deal. My client was a fool for not taking it right away.

I had a feeling my client had delayed his decision because he wanted to continue bargaining in the morning.

Frank wasn't going to budge another inch. I knew. He knew it.

My client didn't believe it.

My office was within walking distance. I liked to walk on the days when I had court because it gave me a chance to make sure I went into battle with a clear head, nevermind the constant exhaust of the busy downtown city street that threatened to choke me and make me regret my decision.

As I approached an alley I heard a man yell. I crept forward and peeked around the wall to see a man at the end of a dead-end alley with his back to me. He had a weapon of some sort pointed at a middle-aged woman who had her back up against the wall.

There was approximately seventy-five feet between them and me.

I had no way of knowing if the man had a gun or a knife, but I knew he had something to make the woman stand with her back to the wall.

I headed into the alley, inching forward a step at a time while keeping a close eye on both the scene and the ground, hoping to get close enough to take the mugger unaware.

I just don't want this to get in the paper. Criminal Defense Attorney Foils Mugger?

No thanks.

Notoriety was always good, but somehow I felt *that* wouldn't be good for my image.

"Give me your purse!" The mugger's voice was rough.

"Over my dead body," said the woman in a calm but terse tone, which was surprising given the situation.

I was halfway through a step when I saw that the light reflected off the ground in front of me.

I was about to step into a puddle.

While I skirted around the water the mugger grabbed the woman's purse and tried to tear it from her hands.

She held onto it with a death grip.

I feared he might indeed take it over her dead body.

"Give it here now!"

The mugger's voice was slurred as if inebriated, which could easily explain his poor decision to pull a fool stunt like this.

"No!"

The mugger yanked the purse away, shoving it underneath his arm.

"The jewelry too!"

"You can have my necklace, but I am not going to give you my wedding ring. Isn't it enough that you've already taken my dignity *and* my purse?"

"Jewelry too. Everything. I want your necklace. I want your ring."

"I will only give you my necklace if you agree to not take my ring."

"Wedding ring too." He waggled something at her that I now identified as a knife.

I took another step forward with mixed feelings, a knife was better than a firearm, but he could still kill me if he had a mind to.

"I'm a widow. My ring is the last thing I have from him because I had to part with all the rest. If you take it from me, I don't know what I'll do. Do you want that on your conscience?"

"This is easy, just give me what I want and you walk away without a problem. Got it?"

The woman's eyes alighted on me when I was less than ten feet away, still creeping up on the man.

"Help me, sir!"

2

I cringed inside as the mugger spun, whipping his knife around while stepping away from the woman. He immediately pointed his knife back towards the woman and shook a fist at me.

"Stay where you are!" the mugger said. "This doesn't involve you."

I could get to him before he attacked the woman but his words also did not sound nearly as slurred as they had a moment ago.

Maybe he wasn't high after all.

"I don't want any trouble," I said with my hands out in front of me and to either side. "I just came to help a woman in distress. I've heard what you've been talking about and I think you've got a pretty good deal. She's willing to give you everything except some old ring that reminds her of a dead husband. I suggest you take what has already been given."

"I need the ring."

I shifted, catching a glance of the ring, and saw that it had a rather large diamond.

I reexamined the woman, expecting to see that her clothes were more elegant than I had first thought, but they were worn around the edges. Her fashion sense seemed to be off by about a decade, my girlfriend Brittany would probably have told me that I was off by a decade or two.

"I think you might be arguing over nothing here," I said, "that's a fake."

The mugger growled and the woman looked affronted by my assessment.

"It looks real enough and I will have it one way or another."

"I have several hundred dollars in cash that I will give you if you let her go. Just let the woman walk away with her wedding ring, nobody has to get hurt. You can leave with plenty of money. Easy peasy."

Easy peasy?

I haven't said anything like that since I was a kid.

"Give me your money now!"

I had to keep from laughing at the hooded mugger, he sounded more desperate by the moment.

"You're not gonna get the money unless you let the woman go. Once she is safely away, I will hand you my wallet. I even have some credit cards in there. Knock yourself out."

The mugger made no move other than a small flick of his wrist with his knife hand which made the woman's eyes grow large.

"Wallet now!"

I shrugged. I didn't like how agitated he was becoming and decided I better give into a demand so he felt like he was in control of the situation.

"I'm gonna give it to you as a sign of good faith. If you let her go, I will sweeten the deal." I reached into my pocket, fished out my wallet and tossed it towards him, intentionally undershooting so it landed halfway in between us. I tried not to flinch when it landed in a puddle.

The man was about to take a step forward when he turned back to the woman, wagging the knife at her. "Ring! Now!"

"No." She thrust her ring hand behind her and made a fist with the other.

3

"Hey Mister Mugger," I said, "how about this, you can follow me to my office and I'll write you a check for several thousand dollars. That'll easily cover the cost of what that ring would be worth if it were real, which it is not."

"We can do that too."

I shook my head, something was wrong with the guy. No thief in his right mind would accept a personal check. My attempt to calm him down by giving in to a demand had not worked, if anything it had sent him the other way.

"That only happens if you let the woman go *with* her ring. I will give you several thousand dollars, you can have my wallet, you can max out my credit cards, let's just make sure everybody leaves here in one piece and goes home tonight, sound like a good plan?"

"After I get the ring."

I suppressed a sigh as I studied the man and reached for my pocket but got only halfway there before he noticed what I was doing.

"You stop right there! Stop moving your hand right now!"

I kept my hand where it was. "I am only trying to sweeten the deal." Before he could say anything more I reached into my pocket and pulled out my phone. I held it up for him to see.

"Mister Mugger, I have a brand-new top of the line iPhone. This is worth at least a thousand dollars. I paid cash, I waited in line for like three hours. These things are hard to find. It is definitely worth as much as that ring if not more. You can take this too if you just let her go. If you don't want it, you can flip it, easily getting at least half that much without trying. You can easily get more if you are patient in how you sell it."

The mugger studied me as I looked at the woman, silently wishing she would just run, he was so focused on me that she could make it away before he knew what she was doing.

The mugger swung his knife around to point it at me.

I looked at the woman.

Now's your chance!

She didn't move.

"How old are you?" I asked. "Eighteen? Nineteen?"

"Stop asking questions!"

"I hate to break it to you but the path you're taking is going nowhere good."

I stared at the woman, hoping she would make a break for it.

"What are you, a priest?"

"No, even better. I'm an attorney, a defense attorney." I studied the man for a long moment to accentuate my next sentence. "I represent people like you, people who step over the line, get caught, and sent to jail."

"An attorney?"

He sneered at me. "I ought to just kill you anyway, the last thing the world needs is another attorney."

I pointed at him. "*That* is what you don't want to do. Murder gets you sent away for a long time. This mugging, assuming you get caught, will set you back a few years because you're armed."

"I don't need advice from you."

"You're either gonna be dead or in jail for life before you're thirty. I think we can do better than that. How about I help you?"

The mugger almost seemed to forget the woman. I made a small motion with my hand, but she did not see it because she was just focused on my face.

Probably still insulted that I called her ring a fake.

While I had never been involved in a mugging before, I had represented many muggers in my time. I also knew a little bit about how to talk to desperate people.

I took a step. "You still haven't picked up my wallet and that's worth real money, how about I give it to you?"

I shuffled forward.

"You stay right where you are!"

I shrugged. "Suit yourself. What are you into? Meth? Cocaine?" I nodded down at my wallet. "There's enough for you to get a good hit. You should just pick that up and run, you need to max out those credit cards as quick as you can. If you do it fast enough you could easily load yourself up with several thousand dollars of merchandise. Assuming you have a good place to unload it, you could get a load of drug money."

"Why do you think I'm doing drugs?"

"Aren't you?" I took another step. "I see this all the time. You're just full of anxiety, desperately seeking for that next hit, willing to do anything for it."

"You don't know me."

"Let's start with your name? What is it?"

"You think I'm stupid?"

"I'm going to call you Jim, sound good Jim?"

"I'm not Jim."

"Okay, Jim, I can help you."

"I don't need help. And I'm not named Jim."

"Think about what you are doing." I tapped the side of my head. "You are trying to rob a woman by the courthouse. You are yelling. The cops are going to notice. You're running out of time. You should run. They could be coming."

"I don't hear nothing!"

"You need to go but before you do I can help you."

"How is this helping?"

"First off, I recommend you lose the knife." I nodded toward a trashcan that was ten feet in front of him. "Walk forward, throw it in the trashcan and I won't tell them that you were ever armed. Sound good, Jim?"

"Shut up!"

I took another step forward. "I don't think you understand. I'm going to make you look sensible to a judge. You were trying to rob a woman because of an addiction you could not control but you started to think straight and realized you needed to change."

"I am not on drugs!"

"I talked sense to you, convinced you to let the woman leave, even giving you money to get you through the night. The judge will buy that."

"What judge?"

"The one you're going to talk to when the cops show up."

There was the sound of tires crunching gravel from behind, but I didn't look back. The car drew the attention of the mugger, his eyes growing big.

"How did the cops get here so quick?"

I would be surprised if it was a police officer.

A suggestion can be a powerful thing.

"Throw your knife in the trashcan! We won't ever tell anybody you were armed, right?"

I looked at the lady. It took a moment but she nodded.

The kid panicked and had started to look for a way over the wall behind him when the car pulled away. I looked back and saw that my assessment was right, it was just some random person who had made a wrong turn and interrupted a mugging.

They decided to bail rather than help.

I didn't blame them.

The kid grabbed the woman by the arm and put the knife to her neck. "Give me the ring or you're gonna regret it."

4

I stepped forward, my wallet was now behind me and the kid was four feet in front of me. The woman's face showed more resolve than before.

Jim needed to cut his losses. She wasn't giving up that ring unless he cut if from her finger. He was agitated, hyperventilating, and looking down the alley as if he expected the cops to come from around the corner at any time.

"This is not worth it," I said to the woman. "You may just want to give him the ring, perhaps the cops can track it down."

The woman didn't move. She wasn't going to give it up, I just needed one glance at her face to know that.

I took another step, the mugger was now so close that I could reach out and touch him. "You really must get going, Jim. The police are gonna be here soon."

"I'll leave as soon as I get that ring."

The kid was like a broken record.

I pulled off my watch and held it out. "Take this instead, nobody's ever going to come after you for it. I won't report you to the police. This is a free gift. Just go."

The mugger did not recognize that the watch was worth anything so I waved it until it was lit by a street light from outside the alley.

He reached for it, taking his hand off of the woman. She acted, stamping down on his foot with her heels, kneeing him in the groin, then kicking off her shoes, and fleeing down the alleyway.

She runs.

Finally.

I tackled him when he tried to chase after her, forcing him down by holding his hands to either side, and putting my knee into his stomach. He had lost control of the knife in the process.

"Wait until she is gone," I said, "then you can go."

5

This was my first good look into the face of the mugger and I realized he was a kid, even younger than eighteen. I shook my head and muttered under my breath, then spoke up louder.

"What are you doing?"

The kid didn't answer. He tried to break free from my grasp but I held him down.

I studied his face, looking into his eyes. They seemed clear to me.

"What's going on here? You don't look high."

In answer, he brought up a knee and hit me in the back of the head, sending me flying. I was up on my feet, but not before he was too. When he moved to run, I got in his way and pushed him back into the wall.

"Tell me why you are doing this."

"I need the money. Okay?"

"You starving?"

"Let me go!"

"A kid like you should be home studying or playing a pickup game of basketball at the gym, not robbing some lady.

"I got a problem to solve. Okay?"

"What's the problem?"

The mugger looked at where the knife had fallen on the ground so I stepped in between to keep him from getting any ideas.

"Tell me why you're doing this. Maybe I can help."

"Nobody ever helped me for nothing."

I held out my watch. "It's a gift. Cost me a couple grand, perhaps you can—"

We both turned at the sound of an engine at the front of the alley. A car had just pulled in.

It was no cop car.

It was a minivan and judging by my limited view of the person behind the wheel, it was the woman.

She hit the gas and hurtled our way.

6

It is amazing what can happen over a short period of time. The wall that had been keeping the woman trapped was now also keeping the mugger trapped, forming a full reversal of the situation. Unfortunately for me, I was caught in the middle, so I couldn't appreciate the irony.

I stepped forward and put my hand out, trusting that the enraged woman would see reason and not run me over to get to the mugger.

She was fifty feet away but didn't stop.

Then she was thirty feet away and still accelerating.

At twenty feet she had finally realized that I was in the way, but was determined to still get him.

Just as I was about to jump, she slammed on the brakes, coming to a halt mere inches away from my knees. In the next moment she was out of the van, charging him with a little-league baseball bat.

I got to her first.

"You don't want to do this. You're just gonna make it worse. I assume you have a kid at home who uses that bat. Is he waiting for you? Will he be concerned if you don't come home tonight because you got arrested for beating up an underage youth?"

"This is self-defense."

I shook my head. "It's not. You are now the aggressor. He's just a kid. It won't go well for you if you attack him."

The woman paused, but only for a moment and made as if to get past me. I stepped into her path.

"Go home. You have your ring. You can just walk away. That's what matters. Just go home."

She raised the bat over her head like she was going to hit me.

"Get out of my way!"

I nodded back at the mugger. "He's just big for his age. He made a mistake."

She was pushing past me when my next statement stopped her cold.

"What if that was your son?"

The mugger was frozen to the wall, hunched over and looking like the kid he was.

"You've done enough. He has learned his lesson. Just go home."

The woman dropped the bat to her side, gave a shake of her head.

"If you ever come at me again..." She trailed off and left the idea unfinished. She retrieved her shoes and got into the car, backed up and left.

I turned to the mugger once she was gone.

"You have a second chance. Don't mess it up."

When he went for his knife, I stepped in front of it.

"Go."

The kid made as if he was going to rush me and I braced myself for the attack, but at the last moment he relaxed, the tension leaking out of him like a deflating balloon.

"Why'd you keep her from attacking me?"

"She would have regretted it."

"Whatever."

As the kid sidled past me, I handed him a business card from my suitcoat.

"What's this for?" He took it. "You want to represent me? I don't see no cops."

I shook my head. "I don't know what kind of trouble you're in but the next time you feel like mugging somebody, come talk to me. I'll figure out a different way to solve your problem."

"Like I'm ever going to call you."

"It's better than the alternative."

My words fell on deaf ears as the kid slunk out of the alleyway. Once he was gone, I picked up the knife and tossed it into the trash.

I then picked up my briefcase, wallet, and slipped my watch back on to my hand. I was on my way back to the office when I got a text from my client.

"Tell him I'll take the offer."

"A wise decision," I sent back. "We'll get it moving."

As I slid my phone into my pocket, I couldn't help but think of the two.

My client and the mugger.

One got away, the other did not.

Until next time, at least.

The Hostage Negotiator

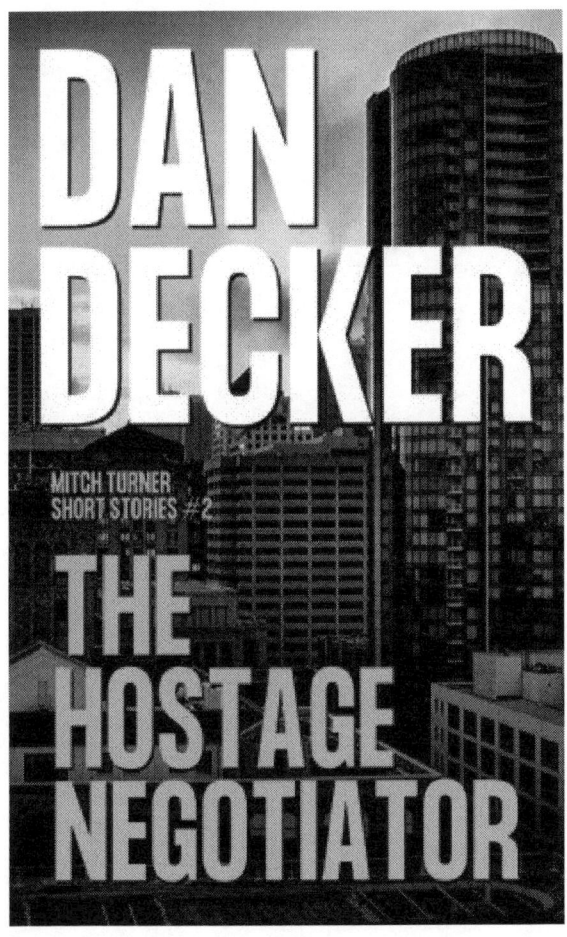

1

The front door to my office opened at the same moment I heard police sirens approaching from outside. I looked out my window and saw an officer pulling into the parking lot with his lights flashing, but thought nothing of it as I returned back to my computer, continuing to work on the motion I was drafting.

When I heard somebody walk in through the front of the lobby I figured that Ellie, my receptionist, would handle it so I did not get up to see what was going on.

Somebody stuck their head into my office.

At first, I thought it was one of my partners or a member of the staff but when I looked up I didn't recognize them.

Where is Ellie? A moment later I remembered. *That's right she has the afternoon off.*

"Can I help you?" I asked the man.

"Yes," the man stepped inside and pointed a gun at me. "I need an attorney."

2

In all my years as practicing as an attorney, I'd never had anybody point a firearm at me. In the back of my mind, I thought that this would be a great story to include in the memoir I was one day going to write, but at the moment, I was perturbed the man had interrupted me because I had a motion I needed to file by 5:00 PM and it was just a little before 4:00 PM.

"I'm sorry," I said to the man, "I don't work under the gun. Literally and figuratively." I motioned to the weapon in his hand. "If you want my help, you have to put that down."

"No."

"I'm sorry, I cannot help you."

The man looked at me as if I were the crazy one. "You don't understand, it is bad, the police are on my tail, they followed me here."

"Then I recommend you turn yourself in. I'm happy to represent you, assuming you can pay me a proper retainer, but I can't promise you that I won't be biased in favor of you going to jail seeing as how you walked into my office and pointed a gun at me." I nodded my head as if coming to a firm conclusion. "Yes, you're probably going to want to seek another attorney, one who you have not held at gunpoint."

"You don't understand, my sister is in trouble. It's her ex-husband, he's coming after her and I had to—"

"That's all well and good, and I understand you have a situation on your hands with your sister, but it looks like you also have a situation if the cops are out there looking for you." I looked out the window and saw another cop car rolling into the parking lot. My office was situated so I did not have a view of the parking lot in front of the building, so I did not know what the police were doing. "How did you get here anyway? On foot?"

The man came forward and put the gun right to my head. "You need to get me out of this situation. I know you can do it. I've seen your signs all over town, you're smart, you're quick, and you can keep them from arresting me. I have to go help my sister."

"Let's say that I want to help you, which I'm not saying that I do, especially because you are pointing a pistol at my head right now, but just for the sake of the argument let's pretend I am going to help you, what part about any of the way you're doing things makes you think that I will want to help?"

"Just go out there," he said, "and tell them that you haven't seen me."

"I can't do that for a whole host of reasons, but let me just give you one. I'm not allowed to lie, especially to a police officer. I could lose my license."

"But you're my attorney, you have to do what I tell you."

"I am no such thing. I made it clear when you walked in that I would not be your attorney until you retained me. Also, I won't be your attorney until you put down the gun."

"You're gonna help me?"

"Yeah, but I need a retainer."

"Okay," the man said reaching into his pocket and pulling out a wad of cash, it was all hundred-dollar bills. I just took a quick glance but there must have been two thousand dollars.

He threw it down on the table. It wasn't the first time I had been paid in cash and wouldn't be the last, I wanted to ask why he walked around with so much money, but it seemed the least important issue of what was going on at the moment.

"Here's my retainer, now are you my attorney?"

I shook my head. "Not yet. You must first put the gun down."

"No."

"Well then, I'm sorry, but I can't help you."

The man took a step closer, pointing the gun right at my head until it was just a few inches away. He then frowned at me, looking as if he expected me to finally cave. "I recommend you reconsider."

"No."

The man shook his head and looked around. "Is there a way out of this room?"

"No, the windows are all sealed."

"Is there a backdoor out of this place?"

"No, but even if there was, I wouldn't tell you."

"But if I put the gun down, you will agree to be my attorney, correct?"

"Yes, in the matter of turning you over to the police, I will be your attorney."

"What if I don't want to go with the police?"

I just looked at him.

"I don't agree to these terms."

"Fine. I nodded towards the door. "The door's that way, I suggest you use it."

"No, now you're my hostage.

3

I laughed. It was surprising that I was handling the situation so well, considering the potential for it to go sideways in a bunch of bad ways, but I was also happy to know that I had the ability within me to deal with conflict even when life and death were on the table.

"What's so funny?"

"You are just not thinking, are you?" I pointed at the door. "The best thing you can do is turn yourself over to the police. If you do, I'll even take back what I said, and I'll represent you, at least through your arraignment, after that, I make no promises."

"But I just gave you two thousand dollars."

"Yeah, that'll get you through the arraignment, maybe a little beyond. If you want me to take your case you are going to have to do better than that, especially when you're moments away from being charged with aggravated kidnapping."

"Kidnapping? Who am I kidnapping?"

"You just called me your hostage."

"I suppose I did," the man said a little glumly. "So you can help me if I put my gun down."

"Yes. I will help you surrender to the police."

"No, unacceptable."

"I don't think you understand, I cannot do anything else until you are in police custody. Once you are, then I can help you. While you are in the active commission of a crime, my hands are tied. I can help you turn yourself into the police, or if you want to walk out the door, I will give you a few seconds before I call the police over and alert them to your presence." I paused as if in thought, even though I was not. "Of course, if you did that, they might open fire because you are armed. They don't like it when armed men try to evade them."

"If I put down my gun, you're my attorney and you have to do what I tell you."

I chuckled. "It doesn't work quite like that. I have to do what you tell me *within* the confines of the law as guided by my own professional judgment."

"Okay, so—"

The front door opened.

"Is anybody here? It's the police."

4

As I walked toward the door, the man followed me with his pistol and pointed it again at my head.

"What are you gonna do?" The man asked in a whisper.

"Don't worry about it," I said in a quiet voice. "You stay right here. I'll be right back."

"No."

I shrugged. "Okay, come with me, if you want, but I don't think it will work out well for you."

"This is a bad situation. This is a bad situation." He grabbed my arm.

I studied him.

"I don't care if you come with me, I don't care if you stay here. It is your choice. However, my choice is to respond to the police." I freed my arm and walked towards the door. He acted as if he were going to say something, but then realized he probably shouldn't, because we were now close enough to my office door that whatever he said would likely be overheard by the cop.

The man gave me a pleading look as I left my office.

"What a day," I mumbled to myself.

When I got to the front door, I noticed that the police officer had waited outside, rather than come inside. The other police car was gone, making me think they didn't know the man they were looking for was here.

I opened the door. "How can I help you?"

"We are looking for an armed man. Have you seen anyone suspicious?"

"I do believe you are referring to my client."

"Your client?"

"Yes, I have just been retained by a man who is looking to turn himself in."

"Perfect. Tell him I will accept his surrender."

"He's not quite ready to do that because he has a concern about his sister and her ex-husband."

"Yes, he mentioned that when I tried to arrest him after pulling him over for speeding."

"You were going to arrest him for speeding?"

"No, it was because he threatened me."

"With a gun?"

"Yes."

"You wait here while I negotiate the terms of his surrender."

"Are you sure you want to walk back in there, sir?"

I paused but only for a second. "I want to peacefully resolve the situation." I smiled at the cop. "Be right back."

5

I walked back into my office, leaving the officer at the front door. "Okay, they're ready to accept your surrender."

"I didn't tell you to do that!"

"No, but you hired me as your attorney, it is my obligation to do what I'm supposed to do, even if you don't think I should do it for you. I'm going to have them help your sister before you turn yourself in. I need details."

"I got a call from her, she said her ex-husband was at the door and that she needed help."

"Did you call the police?"

"No."

"Did she call the police?"

"No."

I nodded. "You just tried to respond to the situation yourself and you were pulled over for speeding. That's for the best because if you would've shown up, you might have ended up with a worse situation."

"Agree to disagree," he said, which was not surprising because people sometimes just got so wrapped up in their emotions it was easy to become blind to the obvious.

"So right now it sounds like the police officer wants to arrest you because you threatened him."

"Correct."

"With a gun."

"Correct."

It was difficult, but I somehow avoided rolling my eyes. "Here is what we're going to do. You're going to surrender and

I'm going to make sure they send somebody over to respond to your sister's situation. Got it?"

"I'll have to think about it."

"As a show of good faith, I want you to give me the gun."

"No."

"You need to do this."

"No."

"If you don't, it's not gonna go over well for you. You must give me your weapon."

"No."

I repressed a sigh. "Let's think about the situation, is the ex-husband still over at your sister's place?"

"As far as I know."

"You need to get somebody over there as soon as possible, correct?"

"Yes."

"Okay, so how are *you* going to do that?"

He didn't answer, he just looked at my window.

"We have to send the police, there is no other option. Before the police will help you, they need to know you're not a danger to anybody else. So here's what I'm gonna do, I am going to convince them to wait to arrest you until your sister safe."

He hesitated but finally nodded. "Okay."

"Give me the gun."

"No."

I put out my hand, took several steps forward, and even though he was almost pointing it at me again, I acted as if I expected him to give it to me without further discussion. I made no attempt to reach for it other than to hold out my hand.

"Your sister's not gonna get any help unless you are no longer a danger to anybody else."

He took a deep breath and put the pistol in my waiting hand.

"I'm trusting you."

"Perfect."

I walked out the door.

6

I hesitated outside my office, looking down at the gun the man had just given to me. Had I really just talked the man into giving up his gun?

Not only that, had I actually taken him on as a client?

I shook my head, wondering what my partner Veronica was going to say about all this.

I looked around for a place to store the gun, but then wondered if it wouldn't be best for all involved if I just turned it over to the officer. I had thought about holding it back, but I decided it was better if it was just gone from my office.

I hesitated but only for a moment. I had not told the man what I was going to do with the weapon, but it was logical to hand it over to the police.

My mouth went dry when I reviewed my conversation with the officer and feared I had shared too much, divulging confidential client communications.

If I ran into any ethical problems, I could always claim the man had retained my services under duress and that a proper client attorney-client relationship had never formed.

I didn't have time to think through all the ramifications and possibilities, but I decided to run with that.

As I approached the door, I held the gun by the butt with a couple fingers, making it obvious to the officer that I was not a threat. When I opened the door, the officer was already wary.

"What are you doing with that?" He asked me, his hand on his own pistol.

"I just got him to give it to me."

"Put that down on the ground."

"Hang on a second," I said.

"No, you hang on, you can't just walk out here with a weapon and expect me to be calm about it.

"That is what you have to do." I stared at the officer and waited. "I just convinced an armed man to give me a gun, a gun that could have done a lot of harm."

I could see on the cop's face that it was anything but okay. I held the gun out. "You can take this."

"Just put it down on the ground, like I first asked."

"Perfect." I put it down on the front step of the office and stepped back. He made as if he were going to go past me to arrest my client, but I put out a hand.

"I'm sorry, you can't go in there. This is private property, you need permission to enter and you don't have it yet."

"Are you kidding me?" The officer licked his lips. "I have probable cause."

"I don't know that you do," I took a step back, pushing into the doorway as I did. If he were to try to get past me now, he would have to forcibly remove me, something that was not a good idea. The optics of the situation would not look good when he was called to account for this to his commanding officer.

"Sheesh, what is it with you guys?" The cop ran his fingers through his hair.

"My client will surrender when he knows his sister is okay. Do you have a problem sending cops over to his sister's place?"

"Are you kidding me?"

"If I were to call in and report that his sister was afraid for her life, wouldn't they send a car to check it out?"

I could tell that I had gotten through to the police officer.

"Just a moment," he said pulling up his radio as he walked away.

I looked down at the gun on the ground and shook my head. I was surprised he hadn't picked that up and put it into an evidence bag first thing, but I had already rattled the guy enough, I was not going to try to tell him how to do his job any more than I already had. It was bad enough that he probably already felt like I was scrutinizing his every last move. A moment later the officer walked back. "I have spoken with dispatch, they are sending somebody over to check out the situation."

"Perfect. I will report this back to my client. Please remember, you do not have an invite to enter this office."

"But I have probable cause—"

"You don't and you also don't have permission."

"That man in there—"

"Has surrendered his weapon," I said cutting him off. "I imagine you would like this situation to look good for you. Is this correct?" I didn't wait I just barreled on. "If you go now, you are going to end up forcing a man from my office who is willing to come along peacefully. I will have a field day with that. Trust me, you don't want to go there."

The officer folded his arms. "I will not wait forever."

"I will tell him that you are checking on his sister, my client will surrender when he knows she is okay."

"You really think he's gonna do that?" The cop did not try to hide his skepticism.

"I guarantee it." I shut and locked the door before he had a chance to respond.

7

"Good news," I said as I walked into my office, staying by the door so I could see the cop through the window. "They are checking on your sister now. We should have word soon enough."

"At last," the man sat in one of my guest chairs and looked more relaxed, but still on edge.

"Let's talk about what we're going to do next."

"What do you mean?"

"After your sister is okay, you're going to surrender to the police."

"No way."

"Yes, you are. You have created a fine situation and the only way you're going to make progress is to willingly surrender."

"No, I'm not gonna do that."

"Yes, you are."

The man gave me a challenging look, and was reaching towards his pocket as if he had something in there. By the size and shape of the bulge I figured he might have a knife. I suppressed a sigh and shook my head as I continued to speak.

"Let's think this through, shall we? If you don't surrender, what's going to happen?"

"I'll go through your window and run away."

"And how far are you gonna get?"

"I can escape."

"The cop has already called in backup. They're gonna be here shortly. Your only choice is to surrender."

"I'm just gonna run."

"Why wait?" I pointed towards the waiting police officer. "There's the door."

The man did not get up and he stared at me for several long moments, fingering whatever was in his pocket. "Tell me why I should surrender?"

"I thought you would never ask." I took a deep breath. "We will tell the court you had temporary insanity because you were so concerned about your sister."

"Temporary insanity?"

"Yes."

"I'm not insane."

"No rational man would do the things you're doing. It will be an easy sell, because it's true."

"You think I'm crazy?" The man rose from his seat.

"I think you're worried about your sister." I looked at him. "You walked into my office, you hired me, you made this my problem, now I'm going to help you resolve this in the best way I can as your zealous representative."

I took a step towards him for emphasis, but not so far that I could not look out the door towards the cop. I wanted to know what he was doing at all times. "If you try to run, what could happen? For one, they could shoot you."

"They are not gonna do that. I'm unarmed."

I gave him a skeptical look. "You don't have any other weapon?"

I stared at his hand where it hovered over his pocket.

He moved it. "I have nothing else. I swear it."

I gave him a skeptical look, and he repeated himself. "Seriously, I'm unarmed."

"I can see the knife in your pocket."

He frowned. "You got me. As long as I don't take it out and threaten anybody, they can't shoot me."

Because you're doing an outstanding job of not threatening people.

"Have you ever watched the news? The police make mistakes." I shook my head. "Now the stupidest thing you could possibly do is to walk out that door with a weapon, or try to slip through the window, thinking that you're gonna do anything other than surrender."

"I could get away."

"You can't. Let's say that they don't kill you, they just capture and arrest you. You know what you've done?" You just made it that much more difficult for me to plead your case.

"I want to tell the judge a good story. The picture I want to paint is that you were temporarily insane because you were so worried about your sister, but the moment you knew things were better, you saw the error of your ways."

"But I don't realize nothing."

"No, you don't," I rubbed the side of my head, "that's why I'm educating you. You're going to realize your mistake once we are done here."

"I don't know, I don't like what you're saying."

"I will present a great case but only if you're gonna walk out that door with your hands held high."

"I don't think I can do that."

"Think about it. I am going to check on your sister." I took a step towards the door. "Don't even think about trying to go through those windows. You won't get far and I will bill you for the damage."

8

The officer's demeanor had not improved in my absence, and it appeared that he was ready to lay into me. I figured he had probably spent the whole time I had been gone thinking of what he was going to say when I returned. As I stepped outside he opened his mouth, but I cut him short.

"He will put on handcuffs." The cop stopped mid-word and looked flabbergasted.

"Really?"

"Only on the condition he knows his sister is okay. Have you had a report yet back on his sister?"

He shook his head.

"I suggest you check on it."

"Hang on."

I waited while the cop walked away, speaking into his radio. I tried to pay attention to what he was saying, keen to see if he was just playing with me or if he had actually done what he said he was going to do.

I could overhear him and the response, but I could not make out individual words.

Several moments later the police officer returned.

"The sister's okay. Police are on-site, and they have the ex-husband in custody."

"Perfect. Just get the sister on the phone, I'm going to have them talk, and then he's gonna come out, and turn himself in."

"We're not going to do that until after he is secured."

"Yes, you are. I want to know for sure that his sister's okay. I don't want this to be some sort of game."

The officer about blew a gasket. "I've been really patient and, as I've already explained, I am well within my rights to walk-in and arrest that man, regardless of whose property he's on."

"I've already informed you of his intent to turn himself in, he's planning to do so, all he needs is a conversation with his sister. Such a small thing to have him peacefully surrender."

"I have been patient long enough—"

"And I am afraid you're feeding me a lie. I need to know firsthand that she is fine, so you're going to get her on the phone."

"You are just wasting our time."

"No, you are wasting *my* time." I resisted telling the police officer that I had a motion I needed to file before the end of the day, because I figured that would make him do everything he could to keep me from getting it done. Not that I didn't think that he wasn't a good person, but sometimes people did irrational things in the heat of the moment.

"You just get his sister on the phone—I don't care how you do it—you get her on the phone and have her tell him that she's all right. After that, my client will surrender to you, easy peasy."

"I appreciate what you're trying to do here—"

"I don't think you do. I've taken on a client in the middle of a hectic day, and you are making my job more difficult than it has to be. If what you've already said is true, we just need a single phone call. This seems like one plus one plus one equals three in your favor. Am I missing something?"

The officer swallowed. "Just a minute. It might take a couple minutes to get her on the phone." It looked like he had added this last bit because he wanted to give himself some room.

I opened my mouth to give him a warning, but then restrained myself after looking at my watch. I had some time, I could be a little patient.

I went back into my office.

9

"I have good news," I said standing in the doorway like I had before so I could keep an eye on the police officer. He was having a heated conversation on his phone and I wished I could overhear what he was saying, but I'd already done what I could.

"What is it?" The man asked when I did not give him the news right away because I was studying the cop.

"Your sister is going to be okay. I'm arranging to have you talk with her now." I leaned forward. "But there's a catch." I waited, for him to ask the inevitable question.

"What is it?"

"You have to be in handcuffs to talk to her. Now—"

"No way."

"I'm sorry, this is a condition for this to move forward. You have to be prepared to turn yourself in the moment you know she's okay. All I have to do is get her on the phone, the officer is working on it now and then we can move onto the next phase of this."

And I can go back to finishing my motion.

"Look—"

"No, you look. You came into my office unannounced. You held me at gunpoint, something that I have neglected to mention to the police officer. I will happily bring this up with him if you don't comply."

"But here's the thing—"

"No, here's the thing," I said, speaking over him once again. "Your sister is just fine. The police got to her. Everything is just fine and as I've already explained, the best choice you can make is to turn yourself in. There's no need for this to get ugly or complicated."

"But—"

"No buts. This is how it is going to be." I nodded to the police officer, who was approaching the door. "I'm coming back with the handcuffs, you're going to put them on, and then you will have a pleasant conversation with your sister."

10

I eased the door shut behind me as I looked into the face of the police officer.

"What is it?" I asked.

"There has been a complication."

I just waited.

The officer swallowed. "Turns out, that his sister..." He trailed off.

"Spit it out man."

"His sister has also been arrested."

"Why?"

"The responding officers found her in a fight with the ex-husband. The only way they were able to restrain them was to arrest them both."

"Are they going to file charges against her?"

"No, they're not. The ex-husband is a different matter."

"You lied to me when you said that everything was fine."

"I didn't have all the facts, there is a difference." The officer spoke with such a righteous look on his face, that I knew the truth.

It had been a lie.

"How long until she's in position to talk?"

"Here's the other thing," the officer licked his lips. "She might be a little unconscious right now."

I struggled to maintain my composure. "Unconscious?"

"There was an accident and she tripped."

I rubbed my hand on the back of my head and growled. "I have just convinced my client to put on handcuffs before he has a conversation with his sister. He is all but prepared to get in that car and go with you."

I looked the police officer direct in the eye. "Do you know how difficult that was to bring about? It took a lot of convincing." I took in a deep breath and let it out slowly. "You are going to have somebody wake the sister. You're going to put her in a comfortable place. You are going to make sure she is no longer handcuffed. And you're going to have her call my cell phone."

I gave the cop a stern look. "You got this?"

"I think we can handle it." He handed me a pair of handcuffs. I told him my cell phone number and went back inside.

11

"I have an update on your sister's situation," I said as I showed him the handcuffs, "but I'm not gonna give it to you until the handcuffs are around both your wrists and I have checked that they are secure."

"No." The man leaned forward. "Information first."

"Handcuffs first. Information second. Phone conversation with your sister third." With my other hand, I pulled out my phone and waved it in the air. "She is going to call any minute now. I'm not going to answer unless you are cuffed."

"I'm sorry about earlier," he said, "I was heated, I was angry."

"I understand."

"I'm sorry about everything. This is just a big mess."

I didn't buy the man's contrition and figured that he was about to make a break for it. He kept looking at my window and the statue I had on my back table, it didn't take a genius to figure out what he was planning.

"The ex-husband has been arrested. They are going to press charges."

The man looked as if he didn't believe that. "That's happened before and here we are again. He was beating her up, wasn't he?"

"I understand that this is an ongoing situation, I get it. It can be hard when you see somebody you love in difficult circumstances. However, the last thing she's going want you to do is to get into more trouble yourself." I motioned at my statue. "And taking that to break the window is not going to make things any better. I have negotiated—and it was not easy, I should add—with the police officer for you to get a phone call from your sister. I have negotiated, for you to surrender yourself, instead of having him busting down the door and coming for you with his gun drawn. I've already told you how we're going to present this whole matter in court. I can't promise you no jail time, but I can certainly promise you far less jail time, if you surrender now then if you don't." The man gave me a steely glare as I slipped my phone back in my pocket and held the handcuffs out with both hands.

I took a step forward. "All you have to do is put this on."

"No. I want to know he is gonna go away for life."

I growled. "That was not part of the deal and there's no way I can negotiate that. Deal stands as it stands."

I took another step towards the man and softened my tone. "It'll be easy. I will be with you every step of the way. Like I said, you're in a bad situation, I get it, this is what I do. I help people in bad situations. Your only way forward is to surrender. It is your only option. If you don't do this, I don't know how else I'm going to help you."

"No."

My phone rang.

"That's your sister." If you want to talk to her, you have to put these on. Now."

The phone rang again.

"Give them to me," the man said.

"Give me a wrist, I will put the first one on myself," I said.

He extended his hand and I clapped the cuff on him and tightened it to make sure it was secure. I then left it dangling, and motioned for him to put the other one on, but he was already taking a swing at me.

Unfortunately, I did not see it coming.

Verbal sparring, I can take all day. Physical violence is something else altogether. He got me right in the eye.

I lunged, pushing him to the floor, and wrapped the other cuff around his wrist. I then picked him up and pushed him against the wall. "I'm not gonna report this to the cops either but you are trying my patience."

The man growled. "You don't want to tell him about how you assaulted me?"

I didn't answer as I took a step back from him, brought out my phone, and held it up. It stopped ringing.

"It's unfortunate that you were not able to talk with your sister. Now, I am a man of my word and I guarantee you will talk to her before the police officer arrests you. Let's go."

12

I opened the door with my client in front of me, his hands extended, showing that he was cuffed. The police officer went to draw his gun, but then saw the situation and stopped.

"The sister tried to call, but we didn't get to it in time." I looked at the cop. "Can you have her call again?"

"Yeah, just a sec." The officer pulled out his phone and walked off.

I waited, looking at the man while also monitoring my phone while trying to not look at my watch. It rang a moment later. I answered and put it on speakerphone.

"Justine?" The man asked. "Is that you?"

"Eric?"

"Yeah."

"They have him custody." She paused. "I heard what you did for me. I really appreciate it. I'm sorry that they're going to arrest you."

"Anything to take care of my little sis."

"I'll come visit."

I disconnected. I didn't want to give her a chance to tell him she had been arrested. I had the bare minimum required to get Eric to go with the police officer. I held a hand up to the cop as he approached.

"One final communication with my client," I said.

The officer stepped back.

"As I've already explained, I've gone to a lot of work to craft a way for you out of this situation with the least amount of time in jail possible. Don't squander it. You go with the police officer. You only say polite things. You only do nice things. You don't give him any information about anything and you let me handle everything."

He said nothing.

I motioned for the officer to come forward, who took Eric by the arm and escorted him to the police car.

Eric looked back at me and said something that shocked me.

"Thank you."

I just nodded. It was surprising to have anybody express gratitude in my line of work.

I returned to my desk, checked the clock, and then went to work on the memo, hoping to finish before my deadline.

The Prosecution's Witness

DAN DECKER

THE PROSECUTION'S WITNESS

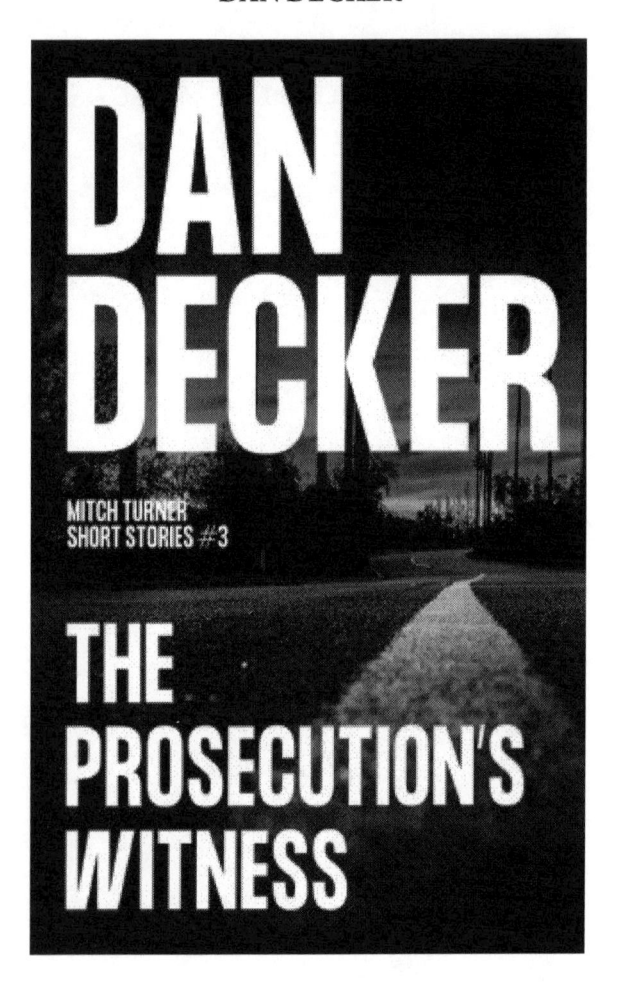

MITCH TURNER SHORT STORIES #3

1

"So, in your estimation," prosecutor Frank Ward said to Doctor Sandra Johnson, an expert witness for the prosecution, "is it your opinion that the defendant was of sound mind on the evening of March 27, excepting, of course, for the fact that he later got high?"

You could've heard a pin drop in the courtroom as all eyes focused on Sandra.

I refrained from glancing over at my client, Mason Smith. I had told him the likely outcome of today's trial and had urged him to take a plea deal, but he had not been willing to consider it.

Despite all evidence the contrary, he continued to insist that he was innocent of the second-degree murder charge.

"Yes," Sandra Johnson said, "that is my official opinion."

Frank's eyes met mine.

"Your witness, Mr. Turner."

2

I studied Sandra Johnson before I stood and addressed the court. "I have no questions for this witness."

A murmur ran through the crowded courtroom as I sat down. I could feel Mason cringing beside me, furious that I had not tried to impeach this witness.

In his opinion, if I didn't take every potential opportunity to protest his innocence, I wasn't doing my job.

He did not understand that it was better to be selective in what you did, especially in front of a jury. The wrong word at the wrong time could sink a case.

Doctor Sandra Johnson's credentials were impeccable. Her presentation was well done, and she came off as smart and informed. I also could not disagree with her assessment of my client's state of mind at the time because our own expert agreed with her.

My client had been of sound mind at the time of the murder.

He had just been higher than a kite.

When I glanced over at Mason, he was visibly frustrated.

Timing is everything, I wanted to say to him, but instead, after a glance at the victim's parents, I faced forward and kept my emotion from leaking through.

Both mother and stepfather had sat right beside each other during the two-day trial. My heart always went out to the victims and their loved ones, even when I was called upon to represent a guilty client. I could not help but wonder what they thought of this whole thing.

Other defense attorneys might criticize me for my empathy, but it was essential to remain in touch with one's humanity.

"You have to do more—" Mason started to say.

"Quiet," I said to him without looking over, wishing Mason would maintain some sense of composure.

I did not like the way the courtroom had responded to my refusal to ask a question, but it had been a gamble either way.

This might, unfortunately, have an indirect effect on the jury but the truth was Mason had been in his right mind that night. There had been no evidence that he was crazy. I wasn't going to waste time and effort on a losing proposition.

I had floated the idea to Frank early on in negotiations that we might use the insanity defense, but I had decided in my final preparations to not bring it into the courtroom because it was a losing argument.

"I don't like how you're handling things," Mason said to me in more of a whisper this time. "I think I might have to fire you."

I shook my head slightly. "The court would never let me out at this point. Not unless you can find compelling evidence that I'm not doing my job. Trust me, the last thing you want me to do right now is try to impeach that psychologist in front of a jury that just hung on her every word. It won't work."

"You better think of something."

3

"The state calls Tony Guerrera to the stand," Frank said after shuffling through his papers back at the prosecution's table and returning to the podium. I could not resist another glance back at the parents of the victim. Tony was their son and stepson. Both Tony and Mason had been present at the time of the victim's murder.

It had been my intention from day one to paint Tony as the alternate suspect, but I had never found convincing evidence that I could present in court, despite having my private investigator spend thousands of dollars looking into it. This was why I had eventually just recommended my client take a plea deal, but he had insisted that he was innocent and refused.

At least I get an opportunity to question Tony Guerrera, I thought.

After Tony was sworn in, Frank started his questioning.

"Can you tell us your whereabouts on the night of March 27 at approximately 6:00 PM in the evening?"

Tony glanced at Mason as he answered. "I was with Mason Smith at dinner. We ate at Denny's that night."

"Just to be sure, can you please point out the person you're talking about?"

Tony pointed at my client. Frank waited a moment to let that sink in with the jury.

"How long did you guys stay at the diner?"

"For approximately an hour and a half."

"Where did you guys go after that?"

"We went to a friend's apartment."

"And who exactly was this *friend*?" Frank asked.

I was surprised at the emphasis Frank put on the word friend. The truth was they had not gone to a friend's apartment.

They had gone to a drug dealer.

"Dwayne Clinton."

"And for what purpose did you go to Mister Clinton's apartment?"

Once again, Tony glanced over at Mason, licked his lips, and then shook his head. He continued with a sigh of resignation. "We went to get drugs."

"What kind of drugs?"

"We were looking for anything he had on hand. We just wanted a little something for fun."

"What did you procure?"

"Some meth."

"Where did you go after that?"

"We went back to my place."

Frank cleared his throat. "When you say your place, do you mean your apartment or someplace else?"

"I mean my parents' home. I don't have an apartment."

"What happened after that?"

"We did the drugs."

Frank paused, looking through his notes, but I knew that he was just giving the judge and jury time to weigh Tony's testimony. Frank had a tricky road to walk because he didn't want to impugn Tony's reputation too much, but at the same time, he wanted to make sure he got the message of my own client's weaknesses to the jury.

I had not been told precisely what Tony's plea bargain was, but I knew that he was going to spend a lot less time in jail than my client.

"Can you tell us what happened next?"

Tony gave an embarrassed shake of his head. "I cannot. I lost consciousness after we got high."

"What is the next thing that you remember?"

I leaned forward, intent on Tony's answer. I didn't believe he was telling the truth about blacking out. Unfortunately, Mason had lost consciousness and was not able to contradict him.

"I remember waking up."

There was something in Tony's eyes that I just did not trust. I knew that he was lying.

"And what did you find upon waking?"

"The body," Tony said matter-of-factly. "That of my sister."

Was that really how you would think of your beloved stepsister?

"Your sister was dead?"

"Yes."

4

As Frank continued his questioning, I focused on Tony, letting my mind tune out Frank's words as I watched Tony's facial expressions.

I had read Tony's report to the police and had interviewed my own client about Tony extensively. At the end of all that, I had a hard time believing that he had blacked out.

According to Mason, the last several times they had got high, Mason had been the one to blackout, and on at least one occasion, Tony had put Mason in a compromising position.

It didn't take a genius to figure out an alternate theory of the case. The problem was coming up with a believable motive for Tony and evidence to back it up.

All of the physical evidence pointed towards my client.

The victim's parents had, of course, refused to meet with my investigator. We also did not have access to the crime scene as it was the parents' home. Everything about this case made me want to negotiate a plea bargain, which was why I hated that we were now at trial.

Tony could've been charged with much worse if he had not agreed to play ball with the prosecution, but as it was, he was their star witness, and the primary reason my client was going to jail.

I broke from my reverie when Frank looked at me.

"Your witness, counselor."

5

"How are you doing today, Tony?" I asked him as a preliminary question once I had arranged my stuff at the lectern.

Tony gave me a dark, indignant look. "I'm at the trial of my sister's murderer, how do you think I'm doing?"

That was more emotion than when you described finding her dead, pal.

"Fair enough," I said without looking over at the jury. It had been a risk, and I wasn't sure that it had paid off. In my closing argument I might make a connection between this answer and the other. I would have to give it careful thought.

Okay, Tony, I thought, *tell me what you know.*

It was strange that Tony would walk free after a slap on the wrist while my client was looking at long years in a cold jail cell, particularly since both of them had "blacked out."

I glanced at the stepfather. *I suppose that's the benefit of being connected to the mayor.* My investigator had looked into that as well but found nothing.

"When you woke up, what was your first thought upon seeing the body of your stepsister?"

Tony stared me. "My first thought was exactly as I had explained to Frank Ward just a moment ago."

"Humor me."

"Mason went too far this time."

"And what makes you say that?"

Tony rolled his eyes. "Mason was always asking her out, but she never agreed to go out with him, did she?"

"So, you figure he killed her while you guys were both high?"

"It looked like that to me."

"I see." I waited expectantly, hoping that Tony would elaborate.

He did.

"He had blood all over him. All over his fingers, underneath his fingernails. He killed her in a fit of rage." Tony hesitated for a moment, and when I saw that he wanted to say something more, I waited still. "In a way, I almost blame myself. If I hadn't come home with the drugs, he would have never killed my sister."

Were those tears in Tony's eyes?

My eyes narrowed. This last part about blaming himself seemed a little too calculated.

I was confident now that Tony murdered his stepsister, but I didn't have any other reason other than my instincts.

Some of the facts as reported by Tony in the police report, had seemed a little convenient and manufactured, but Tony had refused to talk with my investigator or me.

"Let's rewind here a moment," I said, "when was the last time Mason asked out your stepsister?"

Tony hesitated and I could see that he was concerned about answering this question.

"I dunno, maybe a month or two before?"

"So, according to you, he waited for a couple of months after being spurned before he finally killed her?"

"I'm not sure how you want me to respond to that."

The prosecutor was on his feet. "Your Honor, is there a real question in there that the witness is expected to answer?"

"Withdrawn," I said without looking over at the judge.

"Have the two of you ever done drugs before that night?"

"Of course, countless times." Tony looked more confident now as if we had veered back into territory with which he was familiar. He had been prepared to emphasize the drug abuse that both he and Mason had engaged in.

A tricky road to travel, Frank.

"And how many of those times did you get high in your parents' home?"

"I dunno, five or six."

"Were you always in the basement?"

"Yes."

"And when was the most recent time prior to your stepsister's murder that you guys snuck into the basement?"

"A week or two before, I think."

"Did you pass out that time?"

"No."

"Did Mason?"

Tony didn't respond right away. He could see where I was going. He had a bit of a deer in the headlights look, which was surprising because he should've anticipated that I would ask about this.

Unless this was something he kept back from the prosecution.

"Yes."

A hushed murmur ran through the crowd, and I hid a pleased smile.

"So, you did not pass out, but Mason did, correct?"

"Yes." His voice was faint now, his confidence crumbling.

"Did you play a practical joke on Mason while he was out?"

"What you mean?"

"Did you put them in some sort of compromising position?"

Tony hesitated and glanced at Mason, having the audacity to look betrayed. I could see Tony trying to decide if it was best for him just to come clean or hide it.

"I did," Tony said at last with great reluctance. "It was a simple joke."

"What did you do?"

"I propped him over the toilet with his head dangling into the bowl." He licked his lips.

"So, before the death of your sister, you actively put Mason into an embarrassing situation, is this correct?"

I expected Frank to find an objection in there somewhere, but he remained silent.

"Yes, that is correct."

"And did you take a picture?"

"Yes."

"Did you share it with anybody?"

"I put it on Facebook."

I nodded and looked at the clock, wishing that it was almost time for a break. I needed a moment to collect my thoughts. I was onto something here and had managed to lay the foundation for what I wanted, but the next steps depended solely on how Tony answered my questions.

My instincts told me I was close, but everything I thought of doing next seemed just like a dead end. I decided to take a step back and focus on the stepsister again.

"Have you ever seen my client exhibit violent tendencies toward your stepsister?"

"No."

There was something there behind his eyes.

Was it because Mason did the opposite?

"How would he treat your stepsister?"

"I dunno, he could not stop thinking about her, I can tell you that for sure."

"Would he open the door for her?"

Tony didn't answer for a long moment. "Yeah, I suppose."

"When she came into the room, would he stand up?"

"I dunno, maybe."

"Did he ever bring her gifts?"

"Yeah, he would give her flowers or candy, stuff like that."

"And she rebuffed all of his attentions?"

"Yeah, she hated that guy."

"How would she treat him?"

"She was nice enough, I guess," Tony said, glancing over at his father and stepmom. He was torn, obviously wanting to represent that Mason had felt spurned by his stepsister, but at the same time, he did not want to paint her in a negative light either.

Careful, Tony, I thought, *I'm going to get you.*

"How did she reject him?"

"I don't know. I was never there when he asked her out."

I nodded. "Okay, what was she like?"

"She was a wonderful woman," he said quickly while avoiding eye contact with his parents. "She was going places. I can tell you that."

"Did you get along with her?"

I could tell that Frank was agitated, but didn't glance over; it was just something I noticed from my peripheral vision.

"Yeah," Tony said, "we got along okay."

"When was the last time you and your stepsister fought?"

"Excuse me? I just told you that we don't fight."

"Come on, you two are siblings. Siblings fight all the time, particularly in blended families. I always fight with my sister. When is the last time you guys argued?"

Tony looked down at his hands. "I don't know."

That was a lie.

"Did you guys fight the day she died?"

"No!"

"What did you guys fight about?"

"Objection," Frank Ward got to his feet slower than I had anticipated, "he's badgering the witness."

"Sustained."

I glanced over at the judge, thinking of requesting a break, but decided against it when I saw the impatient look on his face and knew that if I was going to get to the truth, it was now or never.

Without glancing over at Mason, without even really knowing what my plan was going to be— something I hated to do, but sometimes found necessary—I continued asking questions about his stepsister. I asked about her favorite hobbies. I asked what she liked to do. I asked a lot of different questions, and then finally I slid in the one question I had not yet asked as casually as I could, hoping to elicit a response from him before he thought about it.

"Did your stepsister ever do drugs?"

Tony swallowed, glanced over his parents, and then shook his head. "No, never."

"Never." I frowned. "She never did drugs with you guys?"

"Never, I resent even the suggestion that she did."

Mason stirred but I did not need to look over at him to know that Tony had lied.

I could stop right here, and then put my client on the stand to have him testify against Tony, but then it would be his word against Tony's word, I didn't like that strategy.

I wanted more.

"Was she in the room with you guys that night you started to do drugs?"

"No!"

"Was she home?"

"I dunno, maybe."

Right there, I had him. I knew the truth beyond a shadow of a doubt.

How did I get him to talk about it?

I flipped through my notes, looking at the workup my private investigator had done for me.

"Did your stepsister have a car?"

He scowled but immediately smoothed his face. "Yes, she did."

"Did you have a car?"

"How's that relevant?"

"Objection," Frank Ward said, getting to his feet. "This is getting ridiculous. Mr. Turner is clearly on a fishing expedition—"

"I want to hear the witness answer the question," the judge said.

Tony hesitated for a long moment, then finally shook his head. "No. My parents refused to let me have a car."

"Why was that?"

"I dunno."

His resentment was obvious.

Motive.

The jurors probably saw it too, but I could not leave it to chance.

"And just why did you resent your stepsister so much? Was it just the car?"

"I didn't resent her. I loved her."

Never before had a statement been uttered where the truth was obviously the opposite.

I didn't even need to glance over at the jury to know that they didn't believe a word he was saying.

"Would it be fair to say that it is primarily your testimony that pins the murder of your stepsister on my client?"

"Excuse me?" Tony said.

"Objection!" Frank said with gusto, leaping to his feet.

"Sustained." The judge looked at me. "Counselor, I recommend you be succinct with your questions."

"Yes, Your Honor."

"Let's start again," I said to Tony. "Are you older than your stepsister?"

"Yeah, a little bit."

"And you graduated from high school before your stepsister died, is that correct?"

"Yes."

The fact I was getting one-word answers now told me that I was getting close to something, and he knew it.

"Your stepsister, she was in her senior year, isn't that so?"

"Yes."

"Was she accepted to college?"

The witness didn't want to answer, but he did.

"Yes. Stanford."

"Are you in college?"

"How is that relevant?"

I glanced over at Frank. He knew where I was going. One glance at Frank's face told me all that I needed to know.

Frank knows the truth too.

I wondered why Frank had not objected to my line of questioning as often as he could have.

I'd taken a bit of leeway with this witness, and Frank had almost sat back and let it happen, only objecting when I started to push beyond bounds.

I gave Tony a curious look. "Are you going to answer the question?"

"No, I'm not in college."

"Did you apply to college?"

Tony snorted. "Like I would get accepted."

"Was Mason accepted to college?"

"Yeah, he is in school."

"But you are not, correct?"

"Yeah, what of it? I'm not the one who murdered my sister. He is!"

I studied Tony for a long moment. "Why do you feel the need to say that *you* did not murder your stepsister?"

Tony was pale now. He hesitated and looked over at Frank Ward as if expecting help from him, but nothing came.

"I... It just came out that way."

"Isn't it true that you killed your stepsister? That you were jealous because your parents treated her better than you? You were jealous that she was going to college and you were not?"

"It wasn't like that—"

"Isn't it true that you killed her in a fit of jealous rage while you were high? And then you came to yourself and realized what you had done, looked over at your passed-out friend, and decided to make it look like he did it?"

"That's not what happ—"

"By your own admission, you had set him up before when he was blackout drunk, didn't you?"

"That's ridiculous! I never would've done anything like that. I loved my sister."

"Isn't it true that you killed her and that my client Mason Smith had nothing to do with it?"

"I didn't kill my sister!" Tony screamed.

The judge banged his gavel. "The witness will please exercise a sense of decorum."

The judge looked over Frank Ward as if expecting an objection, but Frank sat there with a grim look as if determined to see this through.

I glanced back at the family and saw that the mother's face was pale, but the stepfather's face was red.

All the pieces clicked together, confirming my suspicions. He was politically active. He was a member of the mayor's same political party.

I now understood why Frank had objected in the way that he had, making sure to make token objections but also making sure that I had a path to the truth.

"Isn't it true that your father's protecting you right now?"

Frank Ward was on his feet. "Objection!"

"He loved her more than me!" Tony's voice was high pitched and angry. I didn't think "her" referred to his stepsister.

"He's not doing this for me. He's doing this for her! He's only protecting me for her!"

Frank Ward hid a satisfied smile as he sat down.

The judge banged his gavel again and then looked at me and then looked at the witness, clearly uncertain what to do next.

I claimed the moment.

"Is it your testimony that you killed your stepsister, and your father helped cover it up?"

Tony hesitated for a long moment. He had slipped up.

He was caught and he knew it.

"He dipped Mason's fingers in her blood."

6

"I have no further questions, Your Honor." I sat down, thrilled and chilled at the same time. I had never before gotten a witness to confess to murder on the stand. This was one story that was for sure going into my memoirs.

"Your Honor," Frank Ward was on his feet, "based on this new admission, I recommend that we adjourn for the day so we can further investigate the matter."

There was something in Frank's voice that almost said that this was what he wanted.

The judge studied me as if considering a rebuke for the way I had acted in his court, but then he shook his head.

"The request is granted." He brought his gavel down. "Court is adjourned."

When I looked over at Mason, he was struggling with conflicting emotions.

He stared at Tony. "I thought he was my friend."

I patted Mason on the shoulder. "It looks like you're getting out of jail, just take consolation in that."

I slipped my binder into my briefcase, glanced over at the stepfather, who was even redder in the face then before. The victim's mother was gone.

The stepfather looked like he wanted to attack me.

I smiled at him as I slipped out of the courtroom without another word, refusing to answer any of the reporters' questions.

The Ghost Suspect

THE GHOST SUSPECT

MITCH TURNER SHORT STORIES #4

DAN DECKER

1

"Thank you for meeting with me," I said to Thomas Warner as I stepped inside his apartment and looked around, my skin crawling because the place was filthy. My client Fred Samuelson had insisted that I speak with Thomas about his case, begging me to go in person, rather than send my investigator.

"Thomas can prove my innocence!" Fred had insisted. Seeing my skeptical look, he went on. "Please, just spend five minutes with him."

I had finally conceded, just before the officer took Fred back to his prison cell.

"I don't intend to take much of your time today," I said to Thomas, "but my client Fred Samuelson wanted me to speak with you."

"Of course, of course, I'm glad you came. I sent Fred that letter weeks ago, it must've taken him forever to get it."

Why didn't Fred mention the letter? I wondered.

It was difficult to not gag as I looked around the apartment. Thomas pointed to a chair and offered me a seat, but after spying a black mark on it that I could not identify, I declined.

"This is about that letter," I said before Thomas could insist again. "I understand you might have seen something on the night of the murder. Can you tell me what you saw?"

Thomas's face became stern. "I can prove that Fred is innocent."

Fred's case was open and shut as far as I was concerned.

The evidence against him was ironclad, and the only thing left to do was convince my client that it was time to negotiate a plea deal. The murder weapon had his fingerprints all over it. I was not gonna get around that.

I stifled an impatient sigh. "What did you see?"

"Fred was set up by a ghost."

2

I almost left right there, but Fred's desperate plea was still fresh in my mind, so I decided to ask a few more questions before I considered this avenue of the investigation closed just so I could report back to Fred that I'd followed through on his request.

I know now why he didn't mention the letter, I thought. *Thomas is crazy.*

And Fred was desperate.

I studied the man in front of me and decided that he was in earnest despite the crazy claim.

"A ghost?" I folded my arms and leaned back against the wall, cringing when I felt something stick to me. I managed to hide my disgust but could not hide my skepticism. "I'm not sure what you know about the court of law, but I certainly can't put you on the stand to testify to that."

Thomas shrugged. "It sounds crazy, but it's true. The night before the police found that poor woman, I saw his dead brother go into Fred's apartment. His name is George Samuelson."

The name rung a bell, but only because Fred talked about him all the time. George had been killed in a car accident several years back. Fred had not been able to get past it and sometimes insisted on talking to me about it, even when I made it clear I had other things to work on, and it was time for me to leave.

I just waited, figuring the look of disbelief on my face was enough.

"I swear to you, it was him!"

"Fred's dead brother was in his apartment?"

"Yes."

"What was he doing?"

Why am I encouraging this man?

"He was rifling around the apartment," Thomas said. "That's when the girl came over."

"Fred's girlfriend?"

"Yes. George killed her."

"How do you know that?"

"I heard them fight, and I heard her scream."

This could have been the break in the case we needed, but for the fact that the witness was accusing a dead man.

"What made you think this man was a ghost?"

"Well, Fred's brother George is dead, isn't he?"

"Could you see through him?"

"No. He was corporeal." Thomas shrugged. "But I know he is dead. I went to the funeral."

Corporeal.

Interesting word to describe a ghost.

"Do you recall if it was an open casket?" I asked.

Thomas shook his head. "Closed. George was so scarred in the accident that they had no other choice."

"After George killed the woman, what did he do next?"

"Nothing, although I think George lit up a cigarette. I smelled smoke after that. Nasty habit."

I avoided a pointed look around at the man's filthy apartment.

"Why didn't you tell this to the police?"

"They never asked me."

"Where were you when this happened?"

"I was sitting out front."

"Did you see George leave?"

"Nope. I came back inside. I didn't want to meet a ghost in person!"

I hesitated and thought about asking him other questions but decided to not waste my time further.

Thomas was crazy.

"Thank you for meeting with me, I appreciate your time."

"I am telling you the truth, Mr. Turner."

"I'm sure you are."

3

After I stepped outside of Thomas Warner's apartment, I looked down the sidewalk to Fred's apartment. Fred was in jail, but I had his key.

I sauntered down and opened the door. I walked in and inhaled deeply, trying to detect if there was any remaining hint of cigarette smoke, but I smelled nothing.

I took another deep breath.

Thomas has lost his marbles, no two ways about it.

I would have to go over the criminal report again, but if I recalled correctly, George's fingerprints *had* been found in the apartment. At the time, I had thought nothing of it because George had been a regular visitor at Fred's place before his death.

How long does a fingerprint last? I wondered. *Particularly in an apartment that has been cleaned many times since George's death?*

Fred was the opposite of Thomas Warner in that way, his apartment was immaculate.

"A ghost," I said to myself. "I finally got the break I needed in the case, and the witness is telling me that my prime suspect is a ghost."

4

After I returned to my office, I leaned back in my chair, and rather than turning on my computer and getting to work, I just sat there in thought. I had heard it all during the time that I had been practicing as a criminal defense attorney.

Or at least I thought I had until today.

This was the first time somebody had fingered a ghost.

"People will say and believe anything."

I was about to turn my attention to another case, but I could not shake Thomas Warner from my mind.

He had been adamant that he was telling me the truth.

"What if he didn't see a ghost?" I mused aloud to myself. "What if he really saw somebody?"

I dialed a number on my phone. A few moments later, Winston, my private investigator, picked it up.

"I need you to look into something for me," I said.

"Which case?"

"The Fred Samuelson one. I just met a man who claimed that he saw the ghost of George Samuelson, Fred's brother, so I want you to take a look into George for me."

"You want me to look for a ghost?"

"Of course not."

I shook my head and could just imagine Winston laughing at me on the other side of the phone line.

"No, I want you to prove to me beyond any shadow of a doubt that the brother is dead and buried in the ground."

"I'll see what I can come up with."

5

Two weeks passed. I had put off talking to Fred about negotiating a plea bargain, primarily because I wanted an opportunity to make sure that my client's brother was actually dead.

Ellie poked her head into my office. "Winston is here to see you."

"Thanks, show him in."

Winston came in with a big smile on his face. "I found your ghost."

"You did?"

"Yep, he's alive and well."

"Really?"

"I dunno what the man's thinking, he's practically hiding in plain sight. It was just a matter of time before somebody else stumbled onto him."

"You mean he's here in the city?"

Winston tossed a manila envelope onto my desk. I opened it and slid out the photos of George.

"Not only that, but he also lives only a block away from his brother's house."

"So, Thomas Warner really saw something that night."

"Yeah, maybe. Do you want me to look into it?"

"As fast as you can."

6

I fiddled with my phone as I waited in my car outside the apartment building. Winston had not yet been able to find any connection between Fred's apartment and George, and we were down to the wire. We did have George's fingerprints in the apartment, but nothing that directly connected him to the murder.

Only the word of a crazy man, I thought, remembering Thomas Warner's claim that it was a ghost.

I was outside the apartment of the so-called dead brother George. I wanted to confirm Winston's report with my own eyes and maybe do a little more than that.

Winston had also helped me affix a wire to my chest.

I was starting to get cold a couple hours later while I waited in the rental car—my own car was far too noticeable—before I saw George coming out of the apartment.

I brought up my binoculars and studied the man's face.

"It's him, no doubt about it," I muttered. "But why fake his death and then murder his brother's girlfriend?"

Fred had not even known the victim at the time of George's death. They had met and started dating later.

"Therein is the rub," Winston said to me through an earbud hidden in my ear. "Are you sure you want to do this? I'm happy to do it myself."

I didn't answer Winston as I pulled the door handle of the car and got out, heading towards George, who was walking in my direction.

I gave him a pleasant smile when we made eye contact.

He then looked away.

"George," I said, acting like I'd just realized who he was, "George Samuelson!"

The man froze like he had been caught trying to rob a bank.

"I thought that was you!" I said while reaching into my pocket for my phone.

"I'm sorry, I'm not sure I know who you are. I believe you have mistaken me for somebody else."

"All I need is your picture."

I snapped a picture and thrust my phone back into my pocket before he could react, all while giving him my best smile.

Without another word, I turned and headed back to the rental car, curious to see how he would respond.

I didn't really need the picture.

It was just bait.

"Hey, wait a second?" George caught up to me. "Can I talk to you? What do you want?"

I stopped, causing him to lurch to a halt.

"Hey, I know you," he said, "you're that attorney who puts his face all over the small billboards around town."

I hope to afford the more expensive ones before long.

"Why did you fake your death?" I asked.

"Excuse me?"

"I know you held your own funeral, but I don't know why?"

I had my theory, but I wasn't going to tell him that all at once.

"You wouldn't understand."

"Try me."

George looked around. "Is there someplace we can talk?"

7

George was seated across from me, sipping on his mug of coffee while I ate a brownie with ice cream on top. We had sat in silence while we waited for our orders. I usually would have already asked a potential suspect a lot of questions, but I was curious about why he wanted to talk to me, so I decided to see how it played out.

Perhaps he thought he could reason with me.

"How did you find me?" George asked after a long sip of his coffee. He seemed surprised by how good it was. That was something I heard a lot when I met somebody here.

"Don't you worry about that. You just tell me what's going on."

"It's complicated."

"I didn't come here to just get two-word statements that don't make any sense. Tell me what's going on."

"Fred Samuelson is not my biological brother. I was adopted."

"I already knew that. How does this relate to you faking your death?"

"The death of our parents hit Fred hard."

I frowned. "So, you decided to help him out by removing the last familial connection he had on this earth?"

George grimaced and took a moment to respond.

"I can see your perspective, and you have a point," he said, "I'm willing to admit that. However, you don't understand what it's been like. He's just been so difficult. I had no other recourse unless I committed suicide. It was either that or murder him."

He studied my face as if to determine what I thought of his explanation.

He wants to see if I'm buying it.

"You could've moved out of state."

"No. I couldn't have." He looked like he was going to say more, but then he stopped himself.

"Why stay here?" I asked. "Why did you get an apartment that was just a block away from him? I'm sorry, I just don't buy that. Care to try again?"

"I still care for him, don't I? He needs somebody to look out for him."

I stared at George with unblinking eyes. I waited until after the silence had gotten awkward.

"Is that why you murdered his girlfriend?" I asked.

"I didn't touch that woman."

"What is this really about?"

"It was a mistake for me to come here."

"Your brother's facing a murder charge. He's going away for life unless I can find a way to prove that you were the one who committed the murder."

"What? I told you, I didn't do this!"

"Don't play coy with me. I can read the truth in your face."

"It breaks my heart that he stabbed that poor girl with a kitchen knife."

My ears perked up.

That was a fact that had been suppressed from the news. I would have to review the news reports on the case, but I was sure it had not yet been published.

Did you get that, Winston? I wondered, trying hard not to look down at my shirt. I'd told him to call the detective on Fred's case if I turned up anything useful.

The detective was Stephanie Gray. A memory from another decade came to mind, but I pushed it away.

The mention of the murder weapon was useful, but it wasn't concrete. It wasn't going to keep Fred out of jail, not by itself.

"Yeah, you seem all broken up about it." I licked my lips and rolled the dice. "We have somebody who saw you there on the night of the murder."

"Impossible."

"Impossible because you didn't do it? Or impossible because nobody saw you?"

George stared at me without responding, his hand with the mug of coffee halfway to his lips, starting to shake.

"I had my investigator look into a few things, and I think I know why you are trying to set your brother up."

"This is ridiculous. I'm going."

I grabbed his hand. "Wait! I know that when Fred's parents died, they left everything to him. They left you with absolutely nothing. Isn't that so?"

George stared at me with wild eyes. "And you think that establishes motive? Come on, I knew about that way in advance. They sat me down and told me they were worried about him, they said they didn't think that he would get far in life without a safety net."

I released his hand and leaned back. "I think I discovered your whole plan. You see, I figured out that the funeral you held was as fake as it comes. It was all one big charade just for your brother. According to the state and city records, you're still very much alive. I even reached out to your employer and verified your employment. Now why would you want the state to think you're alive?"

I motioned to a man in a hat at the back of the restaurant. He approached and looked down at George.

"Hello, brother."

8

George swallowed and looked like I had somehow betrayed him.

You have no idea, I thought.

George looked like he was caught, but then I could see his mind working hard. A tapping sound came from under the table, and I noticed that his foot was moving faster than a running man.

You didn't expect to be confronted like this, did you?

I couldn't read his mind, but I assumed he was trying hard to come up with a probable explanation for his actions.

"Fred!" George stood with a huge smile and outstretched arms.

Fred stepped back. "Don't you Fred me! I thought you were dead. I cried at your funeral. How about you sit down? You have some explaining to do."

George hesitated and crouched but didn't look down. I tensed up, afraid that he might attack Fred.

"I know what you're thinking, you think that I faked my death, so I must've killed your girlfriend too."

George looked between me, Fred, and the door, and then, just when he looked like he was about to bolt, I took another risk.

"The police are waiting out there for you, George."

9

The table was quiet.

"Impossible," George said while looking at the door.

"The detective responsible for investigating Fred's case is two minutes away," I said, "by now she knows everything you've done." If Winston had not yet called her, that was his cue. "The only thing I haven't told her is why you did it."

"I didn't do anything! How many times do I have to tell you that?"

"Of course, you did it." I looked at Fred. "Have you figured it out yet?"

Fred shook his head. "No. I'm at a complete loss. Jealousy maybe?"

"There is a clause in your parent's trust that if you go to jail or die," I said quietly, "George becomes the primary beneficiary."

One moment everything was fine. The next Fred lunged at George.

I pulled Fred off and got in between the two.

The door to the diner open and Stephanie Gray came in with a couple of uniformed cops behind her.

George looked like he was going to run, but Stephanie pulled out her pistol and pointed it at him before he could act. The other officers followed suit.

"Hands in the air where I can see them!"

At first, it looked like George was not going to respond, as if he was considering suicide by cop. He glanced over at Fred and then back at me, before he thrust his hands up into the air and was taken into custody.

"Did Winston get you everything?" I asked Stephanie.

"Yep."

Her face was grim, but that was her usual expression when she saw me. It had been years since she'd dumped me in law school, but whenever I saw her, it was like it had just happened yesterday. Without another word to me, she left with George in tow, reading him his rights as she went.

"I'll reach out to Frank Ward to get the charges against you dropped," I said to Fred, as I sunk back down to finish my brownie and ice cream.

It had never tasted better.

The Good Client

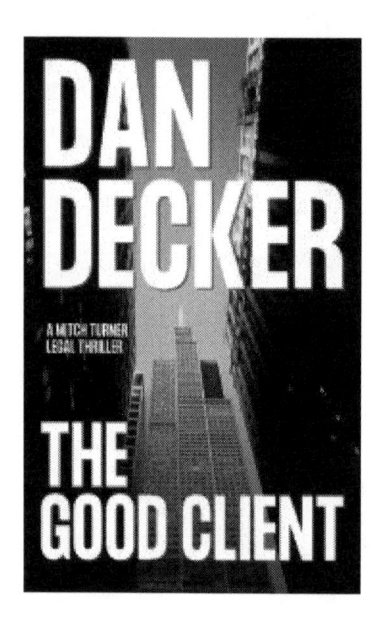

Criminal defense attorney Mitch Turner is awoken in the middle of the night by a message from his nerdy law school employee, Timothy Cooper, begging Mitch for help. Uncertain about the problem from Timothy's cryptic texts, Mitch Turner slips into his suit and heads over to visit Timothy, unable to imagine any reason why Timothy would be calling for help at such a late hour. Mitch arrives to find the police at Timothy's apartment and learns that Timothy's roommate was murdered.

Mitch immediately retrieves Timothy from the police before they can get him to say anything more and while in the process has a run-in with his ex-girlfriend who is now a detective. Mitch takes Timothy back to his office to debrief, but not long afterward, the police show up and arrest Timothy for the murder of his roommate.

There are no witnesses. There are no other suspects.

The police consider it an open and shut case, but the only thing that keeps Mitch from arranging a plea bargain is his belief that his client did not do it. The deeper Mitch digs, the more he learns that his client has secrets that he wants to be kept quiet at any cost, even at the expense of going to jail for something he did not do. Mitch soon learns he must work at odds with his client to provide the best legal representation possible, going around Timothy as he fights to keep his client out of jail.

If you like legal thrillers, this novel is for you. Mitch Turner is a fast-talking lawyer who takes risks where others might not. Fans of John Grisham, Michael Connelly, and Scott Turrow will enjoy this story. Pick up your copy today![1]

---

1. https://www.amazon.com/Good-Client-Dan-Decker-ebook/dp/B083ZLN-MW8/

Author's Note

If you would like to receive notifications about other upcoming works, sneak peeks, and other extras, go to dandeckerbooks.com[1] and sign up for my newsletter. Finally, if you would like to reach out, please feel free to drop me a line at dan@dandeckerbooks.com. I always enjoy hearing from readers.

---

1. http://www.dandeckerbooks.com/

Books by Dan Decker

Science Fiction & Fantasy

The Red Survivor Chronicles
Red Survivor[1]
The Sawyer Gambit[2]
The Assassin in the Hold
The McClellan Colony
The Phantom Torpedoes
The Ambush on Kural 2

Monster Country:
Vince Carter Chronicles
Monster Country: Genizyz[3]

Monster Country:
Parry Peter Chronicles
Monster Country: Recruit (Novella)[4]
Monster Country: Delivery (Novella)[5]

---

1. http://www.dandeckerbooks.com/red-survivor/

2. http://www.dandeckerbooks.com/the-sawyer-gambit/

3. http://www.dandeckerbooks.com/monster-country-genizyz/

4. http://www.dandeckerbooks.com/monster-country-recruit/

5. http://www.dandeckerbooks.com/monster-country-recruit/

Dead Man's War
#1: Dead Man's Game[6]
#2: Dead Man's Fear[7]

War of the Fathers Universe
Prequel: Blood of the Redd Guard[8]
Volume One: War of the Fathers[9]
Volume Two: Lord of the Inferno[10]
Volume Three: Enemy in the Shadows[11]
East Wind (Short Story)

The Containment Team
Volume One: Ready Shooter[12]
Volume Two: Hybrid Hotel[13]

Thrillers

---

6. http://www.dandeckerbooks.com/dead-mans-game-2/

7. http://www.dandeckerbooks.com/dead-mans-fear/

8. http://www.dandeckerbooks.com/blood-of-the-redd-guard/

9. http://www.dandeckerbooks.com/war-of-the-fathers/

10. http://www.dandeckerbooks.com/lord-of-the-inferno/

11. http://www.dandeckerbooks.com/enemy-in-the-shadows/

12. http://www.dandeckerbooks.com/ready-shooter/

13. http://www.dandeckerbooks.com/hybrid-hotel/

Jake Ramsey Thrillers
Black Brick[14]
Dark Spectrum[15]
Blood Games[16]
Silent Warehouse (Short Story)
Nameless Man (Short Story)
Money Games (Short Story)

Mitch Turner Legal Thrillers
The Good Client[17]
The Mugger (Short Story)[18]
The Hostage Negotiator (Short Story)

Other Short Stories:
Monkey House[19]
The Hikers[20]
Exit[21]
Grizzly Wolf[22]

---

14. http://www.dandeckerbooks.com/black-brick/

15. http://www.dandeckerbooks.com/dark-spectrum/

16. http://www.dandeckerbooks.com/blood-games/

17. http://www.dandeckerbooks.com/the-good-client/

18. http://www.dandeckerbooks.com/the-mugger/

19. http://www.dandeckerbooks.com/monkey-house/

20. http://www.dandeckerbooks.com/the-hikers/

21. http://www.dandeckerbooks.com/exit/

22. http://www.dandeckerbooks.com/grizzly-wolf/

About the Author

Dan Decker lives in Utah with his family. He has a law degree and spends as much time as he can outdoors. You can learn more about upcoming novels at dandeckerbooks.com[1].

---

1. http://www.dandeckerbooks.com/

Made in the USA
Columbia, SC
20 October 2023